AXEL SCHEFFLER

Mother Goose's Playtime Rhymes

With stories by Alison Green

MACMILLAN CHILDREN'S BOOKS

First published 2006 in *Mother Goose's Nursery Rhymes* by Macmillan Children's Books
This collection published 2008 by Macmillan Children's Books
a division of Macmillan Publishers Limited
The Macmillan Building, 4 Crinan Street, London N1 9XW
Basingstoke and Oxford
Associated companies throughout the world
www.panmacmillan.com

ISBN: 978-0-230-01813-6

1 3 5 7 9 8 6 4 2

A CIP catalogue record for this book is available from the British Library.

Printed in Belgium

Contents

Introduction

Once upon a time there was a mother goose who laid three eggs. A little while later her goslings, Boo, Lucy and Small, hatched out.

Boo had big flat feet and was very noisy, and Lucy was almost as noisy, with flappy wings. The last one to hatch out was Small, who was shy and dreamy. Mother Goose was very proud of her three little goslings.

Like all goslings, Boo, Lucy and Small had a lot to learn. Mother Goose taught them to swim and to fly, to count lambs and to waddle along nicely behind her. But there was plenty of time for playing, too. Sometimes they played chase (Boo was the fastest runner) or had swimming races, and they all loved splashing in puddles. Mother Goose had her wings full keeping up with her family!

But no matter what games they played, the goslings all thought that one of the best things about playtime was when Mother Goose told them some of her favourite rhymes.

Some of the rhymes were silly, some were noisy and lots were good for joining in with. So, whenever the goslings argued about what to play or splashed each other too boisterously Mother Goose would tell them a rhyme and then everyone was happy again.

Mother Goose's rhymes were such a success that it wasn't long before other mother geese started telling the rhymes to their own goslings, and now they are gathered together in this book for children everywhere to enjoy.

Georgie Porgie

Georgie Porgie, pudding and pie,
Kissed the girls and made them cry;
When the boys came out to play,
Georgie Porgie ran away.

Jack and Jill

Jack and Jill went up the hill
    To fetch a pail of water;
Jack fell down and broke his crown,
    And Jill came tumbling after.

Little Jack Horner

Little Jack Horner
Sat in the corner,
Eating a Christmas pie;
He put in his thumb,
And pulled out a plum,
And said, What a good boy am I!

"I wouldn't kiss girls," said Boo. "Kissing's yucky."

"You kiss Mummy," said Lucy. "You kiss her goodnight every night."

"That's different," said Boo. "I wouldn't kiss *you*."

"Well I'll just have to kiss *you,* then," said Lucy.

"Oh, no, you won't!" shouted Boo, and he ran off and hid in an old bucket.

"I'm still going to kiss you," said Lucy, and she started kissing the bucket.

"Mummy!" cried Boo. "Lucy's kissing the bucket!"

"Don't kiss the bucket, Lucy," said Mother Goose. "You don't know where it's been."

"But Boo won't come out," said Lucy.

"He doesn't want to be kissed, darling," said Mother Goose. "Boo, come out, now, and we'll all sing a playing rhyme together."

So they sang *Boys and Girls, Come Out to Play . . .*

Boys and Girls, Come Out to Play

Boys and girls, come out to play,
The moon doth shine as bright as day.
Leave your supper and leave your sleep,
And join your playfellows in the street.
Come with a whoop and come with a call,
Come with a good will or not at all.
Up the ladder and down the wall,
A half-penny loaf will serve us all;
You find milk, and I'll find flour,
And we'll have a pudding in half an hour.

Cock-a-doodle-doo!

Cock-a-doodle-doo!
My dame has lost her shoe,
My master's lost his fiddling stick,
And knows not what to do.

Old King Cole

Old King Cole was a merry old soul,
And a merry old soul was he;
He called for his pipe,
And he called for his bowl,
And he called for his fiddlers three.

Each fiddler he had a fiddle,
And the fiddles went tweedle-dee;
Oh, there's none so rare as can compare
With King Cole and his fiddlers three.

The goslings were not waddling nicely. Boo kept tickling Lucy, Lucy kept nipping Small's tail, Small kept tripping over his feet, and they all kept falling over in heaps of giggles.

"I don't know what's wrong with you today," said Mother Goose. "You're all just being silly."

"I'm not being silly," said Lucy, lying on her back and waving her feet in the air.

"Neither are we!" said Small and Boo, copying Lucy.

"Right," said Mother Goose. "This should make you behave. We're going to sing a marching song, and I want you all to act like soldiers."

"Oh, yes!" cried the goslings. They jumped to their feet and marched along, as Mother Goose sang *The Grand Old Duke of York . . .*

The Grand Old Duke of York

Oh, the grand old Duke of York,
He had ten thousand men;
He marched them up to the top of the hill,
And he marched them down again.
And when they were up, they were up,
And when they were down, they were down,
And when they were only halfway up,
They were neither up nor down.

Hickory, Dickory, Dock

Hickory, dickory, dock,
The mouse ran up the clock.
    The clock struck one,
    The mouse ran down,
Hickory, dickory, dock.

Horsey, Horsey

Horsey, horsey, don't you stop,
Just let your feet go clippety-clop;
Your tail goes swish, and the wheels go round –
Giddy-up, you're homeward bound!

It was lunchtime, but Lucy was galloping up and down.

"Look, Mummy!" she called. "I'm being a horsey!"

"Giddy-up, dear," said Mother Goose. "Then come and eat grass with the rest of us."

"My feet are going clippety-clop!" shouted Lucy.

"Sounds more like flappety-flap to me," said Boo.

"I'm going to go really fast!" said Lucy.

"Watch where you're going," said Mother Goose, but Lucy ran straight into the river.

"Lucy's gone clippety-splosh!" said Small.

"Look, Mummy!" giggled Lucy. "I'm being a sea-horsey!"

"All right," laughed Mother Goose. "How about this for a new rhyme:

"Goosey-Lucy, don't you stop,
Just let your feet go clippety-splosh,
Your tail goes waggle and your wings go flap,
Now eat your lunch and have a nap!"

I Had a Little Horse

I had a little horse,
His name was Dappled Grey.
His head was made of gingerbread,
His tail was made of hay.
He could amble, he could trot,
He could carry the mustard pot,
He could amble, he could trot,
Through the old Town of Windsor.

The Queen of Hearts

The Queen of Hearts
She made some tarts,
All on a summer's day;
The Knave of Hearts
He stole the tarts,
And took them clean away.

The King of Hearts
Called for the tarts,
And beat the Knave full sore;
The Knave of Hearts
Brought back the tarts,
And vowed he'd steal no more.

Jack Be Nimble

Jack be nimble,
Jack be quick,
Jack jump over
The candlestick.

"I could jump over a candlestick," said Boo.

"So could I," said Small.

"You couldn't," said Boo. "You can't jump over anything."

"Yes, I can!" said Small, and he started to cry.

"Jump over that puddle, then," said Boo.

Small waddled slowly up to the puddle and stopped.

"See," said Boo. "You can't."

"I don't want to jump," said Small. "I want to look at the clouds."

"The clouds are in the sky, silly," said Boo.

"No, they're not," said Small. "They're in the puddle."

Boo looked at the puddle. "Oh!" he said. "Are there always clouds in the puddles?"

"Yes," said Small. "But they go away if you splash them."

"I won't splash, then," said Boo.

And they stared at the clouds in the puddle until Mother Goose called them over for tea.

Mary, Mary, Quite Contrary

Mary, Mary, quite contrary,
    How does your garden grow?
With silver bells and cockle shells,
    And pretty maids all in a row.

As I Went to Bonner

As I went to Bonner,
I met a pig
Without a wig,
Upon my word and honour.

To Market, To Market

To market, to market, to buy a fat pig,
Home again, home again, jiggety-jig;
To market, to market, to buy a fat hog,
Home again, home again, jiggety-jog.

To market, to market,
To buy a plum bun:
Home again, home again,
Market is done.

Sing a Song of Sixpence

Sing a song of sixpence,
    A pocket full of rye;
Four and twenty blackbirds,
    Baked in a pie.

When the pie was opened,
    The birds began to sing;
Was not that a dainty dish,
    To set before the king?

Mother Goose was teaching the goslings how to count.

"If I have three eggs, and two of them hatch, how many eggs have I got left? Small?"

But Small was looking at the lambs in the field. "Look, Mummy!" he said. "That lamb's got a wiggly tail."

"So has that one," said Lucy.

"That makes two lambs with wiggly tails," said Boo.

"That's right, Boo," said Mother Goose. "I'm glad one of you can count."

"I can count!" said Small.

"Go on, then," said Mother Goose.

"One lamb, two lambs," said Small.

"Can you count the trees?" asked Mother Goose.

"No," said Small. "Just the lambs."

"Can we have a rhyme about a lamb, please, Mummy?" asked Lucy.

"All right, then," sighed Mother Goose. "Then we really must do some more counting."

Mary Had a Little Lamb

Mary had a little lamb,
Its fleece was white as snow;
And everywhere that Mary went
The lamb was sure to go.

It followed her to school one day,
That was against the rule;
It made the children laugh and play
To see a lamb at school.

Baa, Baa, Black Sheep

Baa, baa, black sheep,
  Have you any wool?
Yes, sir, yes, sir,
  Three bags full;
One for the master,
  And one for the dame,
And one for the little boy
  Who lives down the lane.

Little Miss Muffet

Little Miss Muffet
Sat on a tuffet,
Eating her curds and whey;
There came a big spider,
Who sat down beside her
And frightened Miss Muffet away.

Humpty Dumpty

Humpty Dumpty sat on a wall,
Humpty Dumpty had a great fall.
    All the king's horses,
    And all the king's men,
Couldn't put Humpty together again.

"Was Humpty Dumpty an egg, Mummy?" asked Boo.

"Yes, he was," said Mother Goose. "But he wasn't a very sensible egg."

"Why?" asked Boo.

"Because he sat on a wall," said Mother Goose. "That's not a safe place for an egg."

"What is a safe place for an egg?" asked Boo.

"In a nest," said Mother Goose. "When you were eggs, I kept you all safe in a nest until you hatched."

"If Humpty Dumpty had hatched, would he have been a goose?" asked Boo.

"I don't think so," said Mother Goose. "He wasn't that sort of egg."

"What sort of egg was he?" asked Boo.

"The sort that wears clothes and sits on a wall," said Mother Goose.

"That's a silly sort of egg," said Boo.

"Yes," said Mother Goose. "It is."

Index of First Lines